RACE AGAINST TIME

Vincent McDonnell

The Collins Press

Published in 2004 by
The Collins Press,
West Link Park,
Doughcloyne,
Wilton,
Cork

© Vincent McDonnell 2004

Vincent McDonnell has asserted his moral right to be identified as author of this work.

British Library Cataloguing in Publication data.

ISBN: 1-903464-62-5

Printed in Malta

ONE

The sleek, red racing car hurtled out of the final turn. When it entered the straight, thirteen-year-old Robbie Scott floored the throttle. The car screamed down the track, its eight-cylinder engine at maximum revs. Robbie was pinned back in his seat by the force of the acceleration, the steering wheel like a live creature in his hands.

He approached Turn One at 100 miles per hour. This was a sweeping right-hander, his favourite turn at the Grange Park racing track. It was here that his skill and bravery excelled. 'You're the fastest and the bravest driver of them all,' his father often said proudly. 'That's what makes champions.'

Robbie fought the steering wheel to take the car into the apex of the turn. When it seemed as if it was too late, he braked. As the rear wheels lost grip and the back end of the car began to slew away, he swung the steering wheel to opposite lock.

The vehicle seemed to float towards the looming tyre barriers. Disaster was surely about to strike. Then the tyres gripped once more. Robbie again floored the throttle. The car shot out of the bend like a red arrow.

Robbie felt a familiar rush of excitement and pleasure as the acceleration pinned him back in his seat. This was why he loved motor racing. There was nothing to match the sheer thrill of taking a racing car into a fast turn and accelerating hard out of it.

Turns Two and Three were tight hairpins. Here, common sense counted for much more than skill. Fully in control, Robbie took the turns without mishap.

So far, the lap was perfect. However, Turn Four held the key. It was a sharp left-hander at the end of the short, second straight. Whoever mastered it stood the best chance of taking pole position for the race.

Robbie approached at over 70 miles per hour. Ahead, another black tyre barrier loomed. But behind this one stood a concrete wall. Just the thought of hitting the wall at such speed unnerved even the best drivers. Only

John Keats, nicknamed 'The Fox', and Robbie's great rival, could match his bravery here.

As usual, Robbie left braking to the last possible moment. Only then did he hit the brake pedal hard. But his foot went straight to the floor, as the pedal gave way. The speed of the car never faltered. Instead, the car hurtled straight on, towards the tyres and that solid concrete wall.

Most drivers would have panicked in this situation. But Robbie Scott was the coolest driver on the track. Now he swung the steering wheel hard left. The tyres screamed in protest, rubber burning as they failed to find grip.

The car slid sideways off the track and into the narrow gravel trap. The gravel would at least slow the car's forward momentum. In the cockpit, Robbie braced himself for the impact.

He struck the tyre barrier side on. Every bone in his body juddered as his head was whipped sideways. But with the whole side of the car striking the barrier, the impact was much reduced. The car did not penetrate the barrier and it did not strike the concrete wall.

Instead, it bounced off the tyres and, spinning about, slewed back into the gravel trap which again slowed its momentum. It came to a stop on the edge of the track and now Robbie closed his eyes and took a deep breath. In his chest, his heart was beating like a drum.

Badly shaken, Robbie was helped from the car by the race marshals. As he was led away, he turned to look back. The mini racing car, half the size of a regular Formula One car, was badly damaged. Robbie shuddered when he realised what could have happened to his legs had he hit the barrier, nose first.

His father rushed to meet him as he returned to the pits. 'Are you all right, Robbie?' he asked, his voice trembling. His face was twisted with anxiety and he was biting his lower lip, a habit he had when he was shocked or worried.

'I'm ... I'm fine, Dad,' Robbie answered. 'But I'm afraid the car's wrecked. I'll have to take the spare. Is ... is it ready?'

'Maybe you shouldn't ...' Bob Scott began, and then stopped himself. 'It will be ready, Robbie,' he said. 'But you can't go out again unless the doctor gives you the OK.'

Many of the other drivers had by now crowded

around. The Fox, so named because of his red hair and wily driving skills, was amongst them. 'I'm glad you're OK, Robbie,' he said. 'It was a pretty bad accident. It only goes to prove you're much too young to be racing in the junior class.'

As always, the reference to his age angered Robbie. He was as tall as The Fox and though only thirteen, he led the Irish under-sixteen Junior Formula Championship known as JFC. There were continuous protests from the older drivers about his taking part, but the rules allowed it.

Entry to this prestigious new motor racing championship was open to the winner of the under-fourteen Irish Karting Championships. Robbie had already been crowned champion the previous year, when he was only twelve, so was fully entitled to race in the JFC. But the other drivers were envious and, embarrassed at being beaten by someone so much younger than themselves, wanted him banned.

Robbie was about to argue with The Fox, who at present held second place in the JFC, when someone caught his arm. He turned to find his good friend, Sammy Pearce, beside him. She was a small and pretty blonde girl, wearing her usual oil-stained overalls. Sammy was regarded as the best kart racer in the country and was tipped for a great future in the sport. But now she looked like a worried child.

'Are you all right, Robbie?' she asked, her blue eyes betraying that worry.

Robbie nodded. He often felt tongue-tied around Sammy, especially if there was an audience about.

'We'd best leave the love-birds alone,' The Fox mocked. He and his cronies sniggered as they strode away.

'I'm going to get him,' Robbie said angrily. 'One of these days, I'll ...'

'Don't be angry,' Sammy said. 'It'll upset your concentration. Remember, you've only got to stay ahead of Keats to be champion.'

Robbie knew she was right. He led the Irish JFC series by 73 points to The Fox's 60. He was almost there. As Irish champion, he could then compete in the JFC World Championships next year. And if he did well there, then maybe he would drive in Formula One some day. He might even be the first Irish Formula One Champion. Then his name would be up there with Hill and

Schumacher.

It was his dream. And there was nothing wrong with dreams. But if dreams were to come true, then he had to stay ahead of The Fox in the final three races of the season, held here at Grange Park this weekend. With this unexpected accident occurring now though, he hadn't even qualified for the first one yet.

'I must go,' he said to Sammy. 'I've got to make some checks on the spare car. It's only got the old engine fitted, so I don't know how fast it will be.'

'Don't worry,' Sammy said, encouragingly. 'You'll do well, even with the old engine. And anyway, you'll soon be able to afford a dozen new engines with your Marana sponsorship deal.'

'There isn't going to be any Marana sponsorship,' Robbie said bitterly. 'Dad isn't going to sign. He's changed his mind.'

'What!' Sammy exclaimed. 'But why? It's the best deal ever. We'd all love to have it. After all, Mr Marana sponsors the Marana Rally Team. They take part in the best rallies all over the world.'

'I know,' Robbie said, his voice angry. 'I've tried to get Dad to see that. But he won't listen. He says he doesn't trust Mr Marana, and that's that.'

'Oh.' Sammy nodded. 'That must be why I saw Mr Marana talking with Mr Keats and ...' She stopped abruptly, seeing the disappointment on Robbie's face. 'It's probably nothing,' she added. 'Maybe they were just talking.'

'No,' Robbie said angrily. 'Keats is signing a sponsorship deal with Marana. The Fox has been boasting about it. If he wins the championship this weekend, Marana will sponsor him.'

'No, you're going to win, Robbie,' Sammy insisted. 'And as champion, you'll get other sponsorship offers. So it's not the end of the world. I'd best go. Good luck, Robbie!'

T W O

Robbie returned to his garage to check the spare car and make sure it was well tuned. He should have had a new spare car with a new engine but money was scarce and they simply couldn't afford it. This was why Robbie had been delighted when Mr Marana had offered the sponsorship.

Mr Marana was a well-known, multi-millionaire from Eastern Europe. He owned numerous businesses, was a keen racing fan and sponsored the Marana Rally Team. The team was in Ireland for the weekend, taking part in the local Castle Cove Rally. But there had been an accident during practice yesterday, and his driver had been injured. Mr Marana had been forced to withdraw his team from the rally as a result.

Whilst in Ireland, Mr Marana then decided to offer

sponsorship to the winner of the Irish JFC Championship. He claimed he wanted to get out of rallying so he could become involved in motor racing instead. As the JFC leader, Robbie, and his father, were approached first and offered sponshorship.

Bob Scott had originally appeared interested in the deal and Robbie was delighted. But Mr Scott had asked for time to think about it. Later, he told Robbie he did not trust Mr Marana and had decided to refuse the offer. Robbie was devastated, even more so when he heard The Fox had been offered the deal and was going to accept.

Robbie decided to put these thoughts from his mind as he checked the car for the qualifying session. He then visited the medical centre at the track and was passed fit to race by the doctor on duty. Now all he had to do was qualify for the afternoon's race.

Once out on the track he drove brilliantly. But the old car was too slow and Robbie had to be satisfied with seventh place on the grid. The Fox had already qualified in pole position.

Robbie knew he could not win the race. The best he could hope for was second or third place. But at least the crashed car, newly repaired and with the new engine, would be ready for tomorrow's race. That was a race he simply had to win.

Sammy's kart race was due to begin after the JFC qualifying session. Once Robbie had taken off his racing gear, he made his way to the edge of the pits to watch. Sammy's father, William Pearce, was already there, seated in his wheelchair. He was a tall man, thin and gaunt, with his daughter's blue eyes. But while Sammy's eyes were alive with merriment, her father's seemed sad and lifeless.

William Pearce had once been a fine racing driver. But an accident had crippled him. Now his dreams of success rested on his daughter. He pushed Sammy hard and many in the sport didn't like him for it. He found it difficult to get sponsorship and barely scraped through from one race to another.

'You were unlucky in qualifying,' Mr Pearce said to Robbie at the pit side. 'It looked like a lack of concentration caused the accident. You shouldn't stay up so late at night, you know.'

'Late!' Robbie exclaimed. 'I was in bed by eleven last night.'

'Must have been your father, then,' Mr Pearce mused. 'I couldn't sleep last night and went outside around two o'clock. There was a chink of light under your garage door. I suppose your father was carrying out some last-minute work on the car.'

Robbie was puzzled by this. His father hadn't said anything about working late last night. The car had already been prepared for today's qualifying session before Robbie went to bed. But Robbie knew his father did worry the night before a race so he'd probably popped out to check something.

Robbie had no time to dwell on this though as the karts set off on the first rolling lap. Sammy, in pole position, led them out. When they approached the start, the flag dropped. Sammy got away swiftly. She was already leading by two kart lengths as they swept into Turn One.

Her kart was old and battered. It should be at the rear of the field. That it was even able to compete, never mind lead the race, was entirely due to Sammy's driving skills. Just now she was the most promising young kart driver in the country.

With two laps to go, Sammy led the race by twenty seconds. Then the accident happened. At the end of the main straight, a back marker spun going into Turn One. Sammy, coming up fast behind the back marker, had to brake hard to avoid a collision. But at that moment her brakes failed. The kart did not falter. Narrowly avoiding the back marker, it hurtled straight on like a missile.

Robbie screamed a useless warning. Then, helpless, he watched the kart strike the kerb at the edge of the track. It seemed to take off like an aircraft. It flew through the air a few feet above the ground before smashing headlong into the tyre barrier.

For a moment Robbie couldn't move. Then, with his heart thumping madly, he ran towards the scene of the accident. Fear gave speed to his legs. He raced along the edge of the track while the other karts slowed down under black flags. The race was being stopped.

When he reached the scene, race marshals had taken Sammy from the wrecked kart. She lay very still by the side of the track. What if she was seriously injured? Robbie thought. What if she was already dead? Terror seized him and he stumbled forward, a cry of anguish on his lips.

THREE

A race marshal was speaking urgently into his radio. A number of other marshals were standing about, looking worried and helpless. Two first aid attendants were checking Sammy. 'Will ... will she be all right?' Robbie asked, looking at the marshals. But they ignored him and he clenched his fists, feeling totally helpless.

The emergency ambulance screamed to a halt beside him. The doctor leapt out and rushed over to attend to Sammy.

Just then Bob Scott appeared, out of breath. He caught Robbie's arm. 'Are you all right, Robbie?' he gasped.

'I'm ... I'm OK,' Robbie managed to say. 'It's just that Sammy ... What if she's ...?' He trailed off, not wanting to put his thoughts into words.

'Don't think that,' Bob Scott said. 'I'd say she's only

shaken up. She'll be fine. You'll see.'

Robbie didn't reply to this. He was thinking of the dangers of motor sport. All those involved knew you could be injured or killed at any time. Less than an hour ago he had been talking to Sammy. And now she might be ... He shook his head, not wanting to face the thought.

Sammy was finally lifted onto a stretcher and placed in the ambulance. The doctor climbed in with her and the ambulance sped away.

'Is she going to be OK?' Bob Scott asked one of the first aid attendants.

The man nodded. 'The crash knocked her out,' he explained. 'But she's come to now. She's a bit groggy, understandably. They're taking her to the hospital as a precaution.'

Robbie sighed with relief and stared at the scene. The front of the kart was a mass of twisted metal. The wheels had been ripped off and the steering wheel was bent sideways. Sammy had been very lucky indeed.

Robbie walked back to the pits with his father. Everyone was subdued and even the spectators were hushed. William Pearce had gone to the hospital with

Sammy and Robbie missed them already. They were his best friends in motor racing and Sammy's encouragement was important to him.

Groups formed to discuss the accident. It seemed Sammy's kart had suffered brake failure. It was exactly what had happened to his own brakes earlier, Robbie realised. It was important they find out what had happened to the braking mechanism, and why both had failed.

An announcement was now made that the JFC race would start in 30 minutes. Had Sammy been seriously injured or killed, the meeting would have been cancelled. But since she was all right, the meeting would go ahead. As Robbie made his way to his garage, he tried to blank the accident from his mind. From now on he must think only of the race.

When the five red lights went out after the formation lap, eighteen cars roared away from the grid. As he screamed into Turn One, a vision of Sammy lying by the track flashed into Robbie's mind. He shook his head to banish it and focused his mind on driving to the best of his ability.

As the race progressed, The Fox drew away from the

field. Meanwhile, Robbie struggled to keep seventh place against the quicker cars. His great skill came to his aid though. Slowly he made progress and as the race entered the final laps, he found himself in fourth place.

He held his fourth position against immense pressure. And then he had a stroke of luck. Smoke billowed from the exhaust of the second-placed car and it coasted to a stop with engine failure. Robbie swept past the stricken car to take third place. Fighting every inch of the way, he held onto third place until the chequered flag waved.

The Fox's win cut Robbie's lead to seven points. Robbie knew he couldn't afford a mistake in the next two races. If he made an error, The Fox would be champion.

Robbie, a real sportsman, congratulated Keats on his win. 'You drove well today,' Robbie said as they shook hands. 'I'd say you'll have a great chance of winning next year's championship.'

'I'm going to win this year,' Keats said confidently. 'I'll easily win the next two races. With twenty more points, no one can beat me.'

'I might have something to say about that,' Robbie said. 'But still, you'll have the Marana sponsorship deal as a consolation.'

The Fox stared at Robbie as if he had struck him. 'There isn't going to be a Marana deal,' he said. Now his voice was bitter.

'But I ... I thought you'd signed,' Robbie said.

The Fox shook his head. 'My Dad wouldn't sign,' he said. 'He says he doesn't trust Mr Marana. The deal's off.'

Robbie could hardly hide his delight. If the deal was off with Keats then there was still a chance he could get the sponsorship himself. If only he could persuade his Dad to accept it. If he did they could have the best cars and best engines. With them, Robbie would be unbeatable. He could even win the JFC World Championship next year.

After speaking to The Fox, Robbie returned to the garage, intending to speak to his father. He would make another attempt to persuade him to change his mind. But he found his father looking extremely worried.

'Look at this master brake cylinder, Robbie,' his father said. 'I replaced the seals last week. Now see them.'

Robbie took the rubber seals. Instead of being soft and flexible, they were hard and cracked. One of them had split. 'That one caused the brake failure,' Bob Scott said.

Robbie shivered as he looked at the damaged seal. It had split under the constant braking and allowed the brake fluid to leak out. That was why the brakes had failed. 'But if you replaced them last week, Dad, how did they get like this so soon?' Robbie asked.

'They didn't get like that in a week,' his father said quietly. 'Those seals are old.'

'But that doesn't make sense,' Robbie said. 'Unless ...' He stopped. 'Do you mean that ... that someone must have tampered with my car? That they ...' Robbie was so horrified, he couldn't even put his thoughts into words.

'I do,' Bob Scott said, his voice hard with anger. 'Someone removed the new seals and fitted these, knowing they'd fail. Whoever it was, they were determined you shouldn't win this weekend.'

'But that's so dangerous,' Robbie said. 'I ... I could have been seriously injured. Or killed.' The thought made him tremble.

Robbie decided to tell his father what William Pearce had said about the light in the garage last night. 'It wasn't me who was in the garage then,' Bob Scott said. 'So it must have been whoever swapped the seals.'

They stared at one another. Both were wondering who might have reason to stop Robbie winning. There was only one person – that was John Keats, The Fox.

Had The Fox or his father swapped the seals last night? Were they so determined to win that they were willing to risk Robbie's life? Did they watch the qualifying session knowing he was going to crash?

Robbie's anger boiled over. He was determined to confront The Fox. But just then his father placed his hand on his son's shoulder. 'Wait, Robbie,' he said. 'We don't have any proof. So don't do anything rash.'

'But ...' Robbie protested, still angry.

'Let's just wait and see,' Bob Scott said. 'Tomorrow is another day. And there's still two races to go. You can still win those and be champion. A lot of good the Marana sponsorship deal will do The Fox then!'

'But they're not signing,' Robbie said. 'The Fox just told me his father won't sign.' Robbie hesitated and then decided this might be the best moment to ask his father about reconsidering his decision. 'We ... we could still get that deal,' Robbie went on. 'It would mean no more money worries for us.'

'No, Robbie.' His father's voice was firm. 'I don't trust

Mr Marana. I never liked the rally team he sponsored. Did you know his rally driver was once in prison for fraud?'

'No,' Robbie said. 'I didn't know that.'

'Well it's true,' Mr Scott told him. 'So I won't have anything to do with him. That's my last word on the subject.'

Robbie knew there was no point arguing further with his father. But, as Sammy had pointed out, if Robbie became JFC champion in two days' time, he would have no shortage of sponsorship offers. All he had to do now was win his last two races and he would be one step closer to attaining his dream.

FOUR

That evening Robbie and his father visited Sammy in the hospital. Robbie was very aware of the smells of disinfectant and sickness there. They reminded him of times he had visited his mother when she was ill. She had died two years ago and he still missed her terribly. She had been his greatest fan and he dearly wanted to be champion for her.

As they passed the cafeteria, they saw William Pearce. He was deep in conversation with Mr Marana. Robbie and his father exchanged glances.

'I wonder what Marana's doing here,' Mr Scott pondered, frowning.

'Maybe he's come to enquire about Sammy,' Robbie suggested.

'I don't think so.' Mr Scott pursed his face. 'I just hope

that William isn't ...' He trailed off as they entered the lift.

'You hope what, Dad?' Robbie asked.

'Nothing, Robbie. Just thinking aloud.' The lift stopped and they both got out.

They found Sammy in a single ward. She looked pale and shaken, but her face lit up when she saw them. 'Robbie!' she said, holding out her hand. Embarrassed, he shook it.

'How are you, Sammy?' Bob Scott asked, as he and Robbie sat down.

'I'm fine,' she said. 'There's nothing really the matter with me. But the doctors insist I have to stay here over night.'

'Quite right,' Mr Scott said. 'It's better to be safe than sorry. You gave us all a terrible fright.'

'I gave myself one too.' She smiled wanly.

Robbie knew she must be feeling lonely and scared. Her father was a gruff man and since his accident he didn't show much emotion. Robbie knew too that Sammy missed her mother also. Her mum had wanted her husband to give up motor racing, but he stubbornly refused to do so.

After the accident, his wife left home. Sammy had felt

betrayed and abandoned and, to compensate, she threw herself wholeheartedly into the sport. Robbie knew it was her way of coping with the pain. Indeed, he himself had used motor racing to help get over the loss of his mother.

'Do you know what happened to your kart?' Robbie now asked. 'What caused the accident?'

'We're not certain yet,' she said. 'But the rear brake disc had a hairline crack. We couldn't afford to replace it. I think it must have shattered.'

'What!' Robbie exclaimed in disbelief. 'You knew about it? But you shouldn't have gone out, Sammy. Your father shouldn't have allowed it. You could have been killed or seriously injured.'

'But I wasn't, was I?'

'That's not the point. You could have borrowed a disc. We have some left over from my karting days.'

'We can't borrow everything, Robbie,' she said. 'Anyway, Dad wouldn't like it. And neither would I.'

'He'd prefer to see you injured. Or dead. Is that it?' Robbie clenched his fists and leaned closer to Sammy.

'Robbie!' his father warned.

'Sorry,' Robbie said. 'I didn't mean ...'

'That's all right, Robbie,' Sammy said. 'I know you're

24

upset. But then, look what happened to you,' she went on. 'You probably have the best-maintained car of all. Yet something broke on that.'

'But that was ...' Robbie began and stopped short as his father took a fit of coughing. Robbie knew this was a warning not to mention the brake seals. Robbie clammed up and took to examining the floor.

'Well, the good news is, you won't have to worry about me any more,' Sammy said. 'Mr Marana has offered us a sponsorship deal. When neither you nor Mr Keats were interested, he came to us. He thinks I could be the Irish JFC Champion next year. He says he thinks I'm good enough to go all the way to the top. Dad's actually signing the deal just now. Isn't that brilliant, Robbie?'

'Sure,' Robbie said, trying to sound happy. He tried to tell himself he was happy, for Sammy's sake. And in a way he was happy for her. But his spirits had been dashed too, if he were honest. Now Sammy had the sponsorship deal, there was no hope of him getting it. His dream of a new spare car and engine was finished.

'It's going to be brilliant,' Sammy went on, her face alight with pleasure. 'Mr Marana is sponsoring me to race in some junior international karting events and next year he'll sponsor me in the Irish JFC competition, if I win the under-fourteen Irish Karting Championship this weekend. He's also going to sponsor me in the junior international karting races next year! They're held at the same venues and times as the World JFC races. So we'll be able to see each other when you're racing abroad, Robbie.'

'I'm not Irish JFC Champion yet,' Robbie said with some bitterness.

'But you will be,' Sammy said. 'You're the best. You'll win your next two races. The Fox doesn't have a chance.'

Her praise cheered Robbie. If he did win the Irish JFC, then he would get other sponsorship. But no other deal would be as good as the deal Mr Marana had offered.

When Mr Pearce came into the ward, they chatted with him but no one mentioned the Marana deal.

'Well, we'd best be getting back,' Mr Scott finally said.

At the ward door Robbie turned back for one last wave. Sammy's pale face seemed lost against the white pillow. A tremor ran through his body as he relived those heart-stopping moments when he saw her lying by the track. If anything had happened to her, he wondered, would he have had the enthusiasm to race again?

Robbie knew that a thin line separated the average driver from the truly great. And while almost anything could destroy a great driver, no power on earth could make the average driver great.

The most likely thing to destroy a great driver was to dwell on the dangers encountered. So Robbie knew he must put such thoughts from his mind for the coming days if he was to drive at his very best.

In the hospital car park they saw Mr Marana talking to another man.

'I know him,' Mr Scott said. 'I've seen him somewhere before. I think his picture was on the paper.' They watched as the man handed Mr Marana a bulky brown envelope. Then they shook hands.

'There's something odd going on,' Mr Scott said, almost to himself, as they reached their car. 'Why would Marana sponsor Sammy in international karting events? It doesn't make sense.'

'To get experience,' Robbie said. 'And anyway, he can afford it.'

'I wonder,' Mr Scott said. 'I just wonder ...'

On the way back to the track they discussed Robbie's chances of winning the next races.

'The car will be perfect,' Bob Scott said. 'It's every bit as good as Keats' car and since you're the better driver ... I think you can do it, Robbie. I think you can win. Then we won't have to worry about money. And we can forget about Mr Marana and his deals.'

'I think I can win too,' Robbie said, 'providing no one interferes with the car.'

'No one will this time,' Bob Scott said grimly. 'I'm sleeping in the garage from now on. We'll see then if The Fox has it all his way.'

'You think it was him?' Robbie asked.

'He's the only one with a motive,' his father said grimly. 'But it's the last time he'll risk your life.'

Robbie realised his father was probably right. But yet he felt troubled. The Fox was bigheaded and irritating at times. But he was a good driver and at heart a good sportsman. Surely he wouldn't have risked injuring or killing a fellow driver, no matter what the reward?

Someone had interfered with the car though. And whoever that was, they had intended injuring the driver. Brake failure almost inevitably leads to injury. Whoever tampered with the car hadn't merely wished to stop Robbie winning this race, but also from winning any other race this season.

The only other driver with a hope of winning the championship was The Fox. It made sense that he, or more likely his father, was the one who had fitted the damaged seals. To do that, they must have been desperate to win the championship and clinch the Marana sponsorship deal.

But then, why had they already turned down the deal? It didn't make sense. Still puzzled, Robbie thrust it from his mind. He must only concentrate on winning his races. If he won tomorrow, he could clinch the championship on Monday.

FIVE

On his way to the pits next morning, Robbie passed Mr Pearce's tent. He heard voices.

'You've signed the deal. You can't back out now.' Robbie recognised the voice. It was Mr Marana and he sounded angry.

Robbie was surprised and puzzled. Why would William Pearce want to back out of the sponsorship deal now? They, above anyone else racing just now, needed the money. It was even more surprising than Mr Keats' decision to turn down the deal.

'But we can't go to France tomorrow, Mr Marana,' William Pearce pleaded. 'Sammy's racing today and tomorrow. If she wins, she'll be the under-fourteen Irish Karting Champion. That means she can race in the JFC series next year. Sure isn't that why you sponsored her?'

'That doesn't matter anymore,' Mr Marana said. 'All that matters is that she goes to France tomorrow. She can get in some practice at the French circuits while she's there.'

'But the Irish Championship,' Mr Pearce began. 'It's her greatest ...'

'Just shut up. I've heard enough excuses for one day.' This was a different man's voice and he sounded even more annoyed than Mr Marana. 'You and your daughter will travel with Mr Marana's new car transporter to France tomorrow. Or else ...'

'Or else what?' Mr Pearce demanded. He now sounded angry. 'Are you threatening me, Bazzer?'

'Take it any way you like,' the man said. 'Just you make sure you're ready to travel tomorrow. That's my final word. Now let's go, Marana. We've things to do.'

'You just clear off,' Mr Pearce shouted. 'And remember, the deal's off. Neither Sammy nor myself are going anywhere. You come round here again and I'll have the police on you.'

Robbie ducked out of sight. From behind Mr Pearce's van he watched Mr Marana and 'Bazzer' emerge from the tent. It was the man he and his father had seen in the hospital car park yesterday evening.

Robbie followed them, taking care not to be seen. They were arguing. 'I'll go and pick up the girl,' he heard Bazzer saying. 'I'll take her to Castle Cove. Then we won't have any more problems.'

'But you can't ...' Mr Marana began.

Bazzer stopped and caught Mr Marana by the lapels of his jacket. 'I'll get the girl,' he said. 'That's my final word on the matter. We made a deal and I want those paintings in France tomorrow. So you just do what you've been paid for.'

Bazzer shook Mr Marana fiercely and they walked on towards the car park. Here they sat into a black Mercedes and roared away.

Puzzled, Robbie turned back. Mr Pearce had wheeled himself almost halfway to the car park. Robbie waved and ran over to him, intending to enquire about Sammy. But Mr Pearce swung his wheelchair about and headed back to his tent.

Robbie shrugged and went on to the pits where his father was making some final checks on the car. 'Are you all right, Robbie?' he asked. 'You look a bit worried.'

'Just pre-race nerves,' Robbie said. He wanted to tell his father what he had seen and heard. But it would only worry him. Anyway, Mr Pearce had told Bazzer and Mr Marana that the deal was off so it didn't really matter now.

After breakfast the circuit became a hive of activity. Most drivers were out for morning practice. The roar of engines and the smell of gasoline hung on the warm air.

Robbie put on his fireproof clothing, racing suit and boots. With helmet and gloves also on, he sat into the car. His father strapped him in and started the engine.

The car vibrated as the engine throbbed. Robbie could feel its immense power. At full throttle, the car was capable of 150 miles per hour. At that speed the thrill and excitement was almost unbearable.

Robbie drove out onto the track. During practice, most drivers were only interested in speed. Robbie though, concentrated on how the car handled. He already knew how fast it could travel. What he wanted was to have it perfectly balanced.

While other cars whizzed past him, Robbie compared the car's performance on the straight and in the turns. He returned to the pits twice to make minor adjustments

to the wings and the suspension. Eventually he was satisfied and completed three quick laps. The car flew like
a bird.

Satisfied, Robbie set off for the motor home to
change and shower. On the way there he saw Mr
Pearce outside his tent, on a mobile phone. He seemed
agitated. Suddenly he flung the phone on the ground
and held his head in his hands.

Alarmed, Robbie ran over. 'What's wrong, Mr
Pearce?' he asked.

'It's Sammy ...' Mr Pearce said. 'She's ... she's ...'

Robbie's heart lurched. What had happened to
Sammy?

'That man Bazzer's taken her,' Mr Pearce told him.

'Taken her?' Robbie echoed, in disbelief. 'Do ... do
you mean, kidnapped her?'

'Yes.' Mr Pearce nodded.

'But why?' Robbie asked. 'Why would he kidnap
Sammy?'

'He's a criminal,' Mr Pearce said. 'He works with
Marana. He wanted me to take some stolen paintings
to France. That's why they wanted to sponsor
Sammy. They were going to conceal the paintings in

the transporter taking her karts and equipment. The police or customs' officers would never suspect a thing.'

'Of course, I knew nothing about that when I signed the deal. But then I saw Bazzer with Marana yesterday evening in the hospital car park, and I knew they were up to no good. I knew Bazzer was a criminal. I recognised him from his photograph in the paper, when he was in court recently. So I told them there and then that I wouldn't have anything to do with their plan. I thought that was an end to it all. But it wasn't,' he added.

Robbie stared at Mr Pearce. It all sounded so crazy. 'Bazzer's desperate,' Mr Pearce went on. 'He's promised some big international criminal he'll have the paintings in France tomorrow. If they're not there, the deal is off and Bazzer will lose a lot of money. That's why he's taken Sammy. He's trying to force me to do what he wants.'

'He's threatened to hurt her if I don't help him. That was him on the phone. He's just taken Sammy from the hospital. He says he won't let her go until I get to France with the stolen paintings.'

Robbie shivered. 'Where are they taking her?' he managed to ask.

Mr Pearce shook his head. 'I don't know,' he said. 'It's rumoured that Bazzer has a secret headquarters somewhere along the coast near here.'

'Castle Cove!' Robbie exclaimed. 'I overheard him saying to Marana he'd get the girl and take her there. I never thought then that it was Sammy he meant. I'll phone the Guards and they'll soon rescue her.'

'No!' Mr Pearce shouted in alarm. 'Bazzer's threatened to harm Sammy if I tell the Guards. We'll have to try and rescue her ourselves.'

Robbie nodded. 'I'll get my Dad. He'll take us.'

Robbie raced back to the pits. It was all a mystery – paintings stolen by Bazzer and Mr Marana offering sponsorship deals in order to get the paintings safely to France. Mr Marana had a rally team, so why not use them to take the paintings?

Robbie put the thoughts from his mind. All that mattered now was that Bazzer had kidnapped Sammy. And she was almost certainly in grave danger. Something had to be done and it seemed as if only he and his father could help. For all he knew, Sammy's life might depend on them right now.

SIX

Within five minutes Robbie, his father and Mr Pearce were heading for Castle Cove in Mr Pearce's van. Both men had wanted Robbie to stay behind to race. But Robbie refused, though he knew The Fox was now certain of winning both the race and probably the championship. But Sammy's safety was more important than anything.

As they drove, Mr Pearce explained a little more of what had happened. 'After Sammy's accident I accepted Marana's sponsorship deal,' he told them. 'I had to, if Sammy was to continue racing. Money was so tight, we couldn't even afford a new brake disc. Sammy was almost killed because of that and I knew we couldn't go on as we were.'

'So when Marana offered me the deal after you and

Keats turned him down, I took it. I must admit I didn't like him or the details of the deal, but I signed for Sammy's sake. Then yesterday evening, when I popped out to the car park, I saw Marana with Bazzer. I knew who he was and I realised something was wrong.'

'When Bazzer left, I confronted Marana, and demanded to know what was going on. He refused to tell me at first. But when I threatened to call off the deal, he admitted everything. He was desperate, and I think he was frightened of Bazzer.'

'Marana told me that he'd been running a smuggling operation for years. He would smuggle anything for a price. That's why he sponsored his rally team. They were the perfect cover for his operation. They could freely travel all over the world without anyone ever suspecting them.'

'But he still has the rally team,' Mr Scott said. 'So why did he need a new team?'

'The police were on to Bazzer,' Mr Pearce went on. 'They knew he'd stolen the paintings and would try to smuggle them out of the country. They were watching him and he led them to Marana, who'd agreed to get the paintings to France. Marana brought his rally team here for the Castle Cove Rally, intending to then travel to a rally in France with the paintings.'

'But now he couldn't do so?' Mr Scott asked.

'Exactly,' Mr Pearce said 'He couldn't use his rally team anymore. Even if he evaded the police here, they would have warned the custom's officials in both Ireland and France to be on the lookout for him. His transporter would have been searched and the paintings discovered. So it was then he had the idea to sponsor a new team. And who would suspect a junior racing team of criminal activity?'

'But wouldn't the police know it was a Marana team,' Robbie said.

'No, Robbie,' Mr Pearce said. 'You see, Marana wasn't going to have his logo on the cars or the transporter. That's what made me really suspicious of the deal. He didn't want anyone, especially the police, to know he was the sponsor.'

They all fell silent. Robbie began to think of Sammy and how scared she must be. He wanted his father to go faster but the roads were narrow and the van wasn't built for speed.

After some miles they saw signs telling them they

were about to enter the area where the Castle Cove Rally was being held. And about a mile further on they came to a roadblock. A rally steward, dressed in a reflective jacket, approached them.

'You can't go through,' he said. 'You'll have to take the diversion or wait two hours until the roads are opened again.'

'But we have to go to Castle Cove,' Mr Pearce shouted. 'My daughter's in danger.'

'Sorry,' the steward said. 'The rally's taking place over these roads and no traffic can be allowed through until the stage finishes.'

Just then a jeep drawing a trailer with a rally car on board drew up, with a screech of tyres. As they swung about to look, Mr Marana leapt from the jeep.

'Open the road,' Mr Marana shouted at the steward. 'Quickly now, there's no time to lose. I must get through to Castle Cove and ...' He stopped, shocked when he recognised the occupants of the van. He clasped his hands to his head in agitation.

'Where's my daughter?' Mr Pearce demanded. He reached through the open passenger window of the van and grabbed Mr Marana. 'What have you done with her?'

'It's Bazzer,' Mr Marana croaked. 'He's ... he's taken her. She's in great danger. I've got to get through to Castle Cove or she'll die.' He glanced at his watch and cried out. 'There's so little time left. Every second ...'

He got no further. Mr Pearce pulled him tighter to the side of the vehicle, squashing him against the door. Mr Marana's breath went out in a wheeze. 'What?' Mr Pearce shouted. 'What ... what do you mean?'

Robbie was trembling. What could Mr Marana mean? Sammy couldn't die. Bazzer wouldn't dream of killing her. Or would he?

'They've ... they've left her in my rally transporter,' Mr Marana croaked. 'It's got a secret compartment and she's locked in there.'

'But where's Bazzer?' Mr Pearce demanded.

'He's been arrested. The police were waiting for them at Bazzer's cottage. It's about ten miles this side of Castle Cove. But the police didn't know that Sammy was hidden in the transporter and Bazzer never said anything about it.'

'But how do you know all this?' Mr Pearce demanded, shaking Mr Marana.

'One of Bazzer's gang managed to escape and he

phoned to tell me what had happened. I begged him to go back and release Sammy, but he was only interested in saving his own skin. As far as I know he's still on the run, probably trying to get back to the city.'

'I was just about to take the rally car here back to the transporter when I heard the news. So I decided to try and reach Sammy myself. But the roads are so narrow and twisting, I just lost so much time ...'

'But Sammy's safe, isn't she, now that Bazzer's been arrested?' Robbie blurted out.

'No, no,' Mr Marana cried, trying to draw in gulps of air. 'You ... you don't understand. The secret compartment's airtight. We tried to smuggle a person once and he almost died. Luckily someone heard him banging on the sides and released him. He was only in there for an hour and he was already going blue from lack of oxygen. So no one could survive in there for more than an hour. That's why I've got to get through. I must get her out. I'm not a killer.'

Robbie's stomach heaved. Sammy was locked in a sealed compartment and her air was running out. If she wasn't released soon she would die.

'She's only got about 30 minutes left,' Mr Marana was saying. 'That's why I've got to get through. If I don't she will die.'

'But we could never get to Castle Cove in 30 minutes,' Mr Scott said. His voice was hardly above a whisper. 'No one could get there in time. Maybe we could phone Castle Cove and get someone to come out to the cottage from there?'

Mr Scott turned to the steward. 'Can you call?' he asked. 'And tell them it's urgent.'

'I can call,' the steward said. 'But it won't do any good. They won't allow any vehicles on this road except rally cars until the stage is over.'

'Then we'll have to force our way through here,' Mr Marana gasped. 'Only there's so little time left.'

'You'll be wasting your time,' the steward insisted. 'And getting into trouble as well. No one can get to that cottage in the time that's left.'

'Robbie could,' Mr Pearce suggested, in a surprising-ly calm voice. He had let go his grip of Mr Marana. 'He's one of the finest drivers in Ireland. If he were to take that rally car there, he could make it. He has to make it, oth-erwise Sammy will die.'

'He can't drive,' the steward protested. 'He's much too young. Anyway, only those who have a racing licence can drive on the closed roads. You'll have to call

the Gardai and see if they can get to the cottage by heli-
copter ...'

'There isn't time.' It was Mr Scott who spoke. There
could be no mistaking the urgency in his voice. 'Robbie
here is a racing driver. And he does have a racing
licence. He has driven in a closed rally before so he
does have experience. I'll go with him so he'll be perfectly safe. Now, that rally car on the trailer belongs to
the Marana Rally Team. They're entitled to take part in
this rally. So if Mr Marana hires Robbie as his driver,
then there's no problem, is there?'

'I don't know ...' The steward frowned.

'A girl's life depends on it,' Mr Scott said quietly. 'Do
you want her death on your conscience?'

The steward looked frightened now. 'Well, if Mr Marana
hires him as his driver, then I suppose it's ...'

He got no further, as Mr Marana pushed him out of the
way. 'Robbie's hired as a driver with my team,' he
screamed. 'Now go. Go! The cottage is on the left, just
over the railway bridge about ten miles on this side of
Castle Cove.'

'Take Sammy's spare helmet,' Mr Pearce told Robbie. 'It'll fit you. There's a couple of others there too. One

of them will fit your father.'

Robbie and his father leapt from the van. They ran to the rear and got the helmets. Having put them on, they clambered into the car on the trailer. Meanwhile, Mr Marana began to unhook the restraints which secured the car on the trailer, while the steward was removing the roadblock.

Once in the car, Robbie and his father strapped themselves in. 'Is the driving position OK, Robbie?' Bob Scott asked.

'Perfect,' Robbie said. 'Mr Marana's driver must be around my height.'

'Great,' Mr Scott said.'Now lets go.'

Robbie started the engine, which fired first time. He then selected first gear. When Mr Marana gave him the thumbs up sign, he gunned the throttle and eased the car off the trailer.

'You've got 22 minutes,' Mr Marana shouted at him through the window. Robbie didn't need reminding of how little time he had left.

Nodding at Mr Marana and taking a deep breath, Robbie floored the throttle. The 300 brake horsepower from the engine spun the rear wheels. Then the tyres gripped and with the stench of burning rubber in the air, the car rocketed away.

SEVEN

The rally car had been set up for a driver who liked under steer. Robbie quickly learned how to handle it and only then did he begin to drive to his full capability. But like all great racing drivers, he knew there were limitations to the speed one could drive at.

Many drivers pushed beyond their own capabilities; or beyond those of the car, tyres, track or conditions. But these drivers didn't last long in the sport. They were often injured in crashes or sacked by the team owner due to their recklessness.

Robbie realised this would have to be the drive of his life if he were to reach Sammy in time. But he would be of no use to Sammy if he crashed because he took risks. This drive called for cool nerves and absolute concentration.

With a feel now for the car, Robbie began to go faster. Soon the hedgerows whizzed by in a blur, the road a tangled black ribbon unfolding before him. Robbie followed its twists and turns, changing up and down the gearbox with absolute precision. His hands moved quickly as they twisted the steering wheel one way and then the other in his fight to keep the car between the banks and out of danger.

He had no navigator to shout what his speed should be, where the turns were or what their nature was, as would happen in an actual rally. But with his father beside him, encouraging him and at the same time urging caution, Robbie felt safe and secure. At times though he came close to disaster, as a bend tightened more than he expected. Then his feet danced between clutch, brake and accelerator to bring the car back from the edge of calamity.

The clock on the dash was a constant reminder of how little time remained. He glanced at it from time to time. Minutes flew by. One by one, Robbie counted them.

Twenty, nineteen, eighteen ... All the time he thought of Sammy and what she must be going through. Each second he lost meant more for her to endure.

He hit a straight section of road and thrust the throttle to the floor. The speedometer crept up to 120 miles per hour. Then, up ahead, the road swung right. Robbie braked hard, changing down through the gears with a speed that defied the eye.

Like a crab, the car slewed sideways into the turn. Tyres screamed as they sought grip. The ground on the left fell away 100 feet. When it seemed they must go over the edge, Robbie turned into the power slide. Now the front wheels pointed towards that sheer drop. Surely nothing could save them from tragedy.

But Robbie was within his limitations. And he had judged the manoeuvre to perfection. Just when it seemed they would slide over the edge, the car straightened and the tyres found grip. Now Robbie floored the throttle again. The rear tyres whimpered, then gripped tight to the tarmac, powering the car out of the bend. They hurtled onwards, a rear tyre spewing mud from the very edge of the soft margin.

'Brilliant driving!' his father shouted down the roar of the engine. 'You're the very best!'

In turn after turn, Robbie's driving skills shone. Once

or twice it seemed nothing could save them. But Robbie had a feel for the car now. Each time, often with mere inches to spare, Robbie kept the car safely on the road.

Adrenaline pumped through his veins. Behind his ribs, his heart beat like a trapped bird. Never in all his time racing had he experienced such tension. No race had ever had such importance. This was one race he mustn't lose.

He didn't even have time to glance at his father. Robbie only had eyes for the road and the clock on the dash. Sixteen minutes ... fifteen ... fourteen ... He pressed on. Eleven minutes ... ten ... nine ... Time was running out. Was he going to make it?

With every consideration for his own and his father's safety, Robbie took the car to its very limits. It was a magnificent machine, the best of its kind, built to be raced to the limit. It responded instantly to the merest flick of the steering wheel. In a power slide, the lightest pressure on the throttle brought instant correcting power. It rode the humps and hollows of the uneven road surface as if it were attached to a rail welded to the tarmacadam.

They struck one particularly bad hump and the car took off and flew through the air, feet above the ground. The engine screamed at full revs as the rear wheels spun wildly.

The car landed on all four wheels, the impact partly cushioned by the excellent suspension. It bounced like a rubber ball, once, twice, and then the tyres fully gripped once more.

The 300 brake horsepower surged through them. Robbie was pinned back in his seat as the car rocketed forward. The rev counter hovered on the edge of the area marked in red. The speedometer moved in a blur to read 70 miles per hour. Then 80 ... 90 ...

Feathering the throttle, Robbie took the next bend. Then up ahead, he spotted another rally car. It should not be there. The car must have suffered a breakdown or else the driver had made a mistake and had gone off the road. Whatever had happened, he was now in their way and travelling at almost full speed.

Despite this, Robbie was catching up with him. He glanced at the clock. Five minutes to go. He had to get past. He hit the horn with the palm of his hand and kept it there. But the car ahead held the centre of the narrow road. There was no room to pass.

Bumper to bumper the two cars raced on. Then, as they roared out of a bend, the road widened a little up

SEVEN

ahead.

'Now, Robbie,' his father shouted. 'Here's your chance to overtake him.' Robbie realised this was probably his only chance to get past. Gritting his teeth, he swung out of the leading car's slipstream.

Down changing a gear, he floored the throttle. The car leapt forward instantly and they drew alongside the leading car. Now mere inches separated them as they raced side by side. The speedometer read 90 miles per hour.

Neck and neck they raced. Up ahead the road was narrowing again. Both cars hurtled towards that single space. But Robbie was gaining. Inch by inch he eased past the other car. Now he was a nose in front. He changed up a gear again and the car surged forward. Robbie was past!

Four minutes to go on the clock. Robbie pressed harder on the throttle. The car seemed to gain speed, though the throttle was already to the floor. Robbie stared at the road ahead. There was so little time left. On the dash the rev counter moved into the red danger area. The engine screamed. The speedometer climbed. 100 ... 110 ... 120 ...

Steam began to billow from beneath the bonnet as

Robbie braked hard for the next bend. As he powered out of it, he saw up ahead the humpbacked bridge over the railway line. They were almost there.

Robbie accelerated again, his foot to the floor. The bridge drew nearer and then was no more than 100 yards away. It was narrow, barely wide enough for the car. If they even brushed the side of the bridge ... the thought of what could happen flicked through Robbie's brain. He shut it out.

Every instinct told him to slow down. 'Slam on the brakes,' his brain screamed. But he knew that if he braked hard now he would lose control at this speed. They would smash into the stone parapet and almost certainly be killed.

What he needed now was what every racing driver needed at the crucial moment – skill and bravery. This was the sort of moment that separated the great from the ordinary. Not lacking in either skill or bravery, Robbie kept his foot hard on the throttle.

'Hold your nerve, Robbie,' his father urged.'You can do it.'

The rev counter was at its limit. The engine still screamed, seemingly now in its death throes. Denser clouds of steam billowed in the air. The speedometer touched 70 ... 75 ...

There were a few spectators left here who watched nervously as the car roared towards the narrow bridge. The less brave among them drew back. Surely no car could leap the hump and survive at this speed?

The car leapt over the hump and rose into the air. It soared like a wingless bird, ten feet above the ground. At the edge of his vision Robbie glimpsed the railway line below him; then the tops of the hedges beyond the bridge; lastly the blurred figures of the spectators.

The car flew on and on. Time slowed down, seemed to stand still. Then the car was falling out of the sky. It would surely smash head first onto the roadway.

But Robbie had judged everything to perfection. The car landed as it should, front wheels first, then the rear wheels following a split second later. The jolt as it land- ed jerked Robbie and his father in their seats. But, held tightly by their safety harnesses, they were in no danger.

The wheels bounced, gripped, bounced again and then gripped tight. Robbie fought the steering wheel, which seemed alive in his hands. The car slewed left and right, but Robbie swung the steering wheel to adjust for the slides and controlled the car perfectly. Fully in control, they went hurtling forward.

Up ahead, Robbie saw the tight turning off for the cottage. He braked hard as he approached and then, judging the moment just right, yanked up the hand-brake. The rear of the car swung out and the front faced into the side road. Flooring the throttle, Robbie surged onto the new road. He spotted the cottage up ahead. The transporter was parked beside it. Two minutes were left on the clock ...

With gravel flying, he skidded to a stop beside the transporter. He hit his harness release and was out of the car in a single bound. He ran to the rear of the trans-porter, swung the doors open and leapt inside.

'Sammy?' he called. 'Sammy? Are you there?' There was only silence.

His heart thumped madly. He had not thought to ask Mr Marana where the secret compartment was located. Where was it? There was hardly a minute left.

He ran up through the long vehicle, staring wildly about. 'Sammy,' he called. 'Sammy! Where are you?' He stopped at the top of the vehicle and heard a thumping sound. It was coming from directly in front of him.

He stared at the spot. Set into the front wall of the transporter was a small panel. He banged on it with his fist. Someone banged back. He had found Sammy. She was alive!

'Hang on, Sammy,' he screamed. 'I'll soon have you out.'

But how did the panel open? There was no visible handle or lock. Desperate, Robbie stared around. Hanging on a rack on the side of the transporter was a selection of tools. Robbie grabbed a heavy hammer. By now his father was running towards him. He didn't speak, but grabbed another hammer.

Robbie swung the hammer and the head bounced off the panel with a ringing sound. Robbie swung again, fear giving his arms strength. Then his father joined him and they swung together. With a click, the spring-loaded panel whipped open.

Sammy was crouched in the cramped space. It was just large enough to hold her. 'Robbie,' she whimpered, her eyes wide in terror.

Robbie held out his hand to her and she gripped it. Then he and his father gently helped her out. She was unsteady on her feet and they supported her as they made their way out of the transporter and into the fresh air.

When Sammy had somewhat recovered from her ordeal, she told them what had happened. Bazzer had come to the hospital that morning, claiming her father had sent him to collect her. She had been discharged and as Bazzer claimed to be working for Mr Marana and knew all about the sponsorship deal, Sammy didn't suspect anything. She left the hospital with him, thinking he was taking her back to Grange Park. But instead he took her here to the cottage, where she was shut up in the secret compartment.

It made Robbie angry to even think about it. But at least Sammy was safe now. That was all that mattered. He had got here just in time to save her.

Soon they heard the wail of a siren. Minutes later a Garda car arrived. Then Mr Pearce arrived in his van. They were followed by other rally enthusiasts. Everyone wanted to know who had driven the Marana Team Car. It had recorded the fastest time ever for the distance from the roadblock to the railway bridge.

Robbie was surrounded. Everyone wanted to shake his hand. 'The finest drive ever,' an organiser said in awe. 'You knocked a whole minute off the record time. And no car has ever been recorded going through the bridge at more than 70 miles per hour. So you've smashed that record too by five miles per hour.'

'You're the finest driver in Ireland,' they told Robbie. 'You'll be a great champion one day.'

Robbie thanked them all for their praise. But he knew it would have meant nothing to him if he hadn't reached Sammy in time. He had done so though and she was fine, thanks to his driving skills.

EIGHT

It was the morning of the third and final race of the championship. John Keats had won the previous day's race and now led Robbie by only three points. Today Keats had only to finish ahead of Robbie to be crowned champion.

The press had gathered at the track from early morning. They wanted to interview the hero and watch him race. By now Mr Marana, Bazzer and their accomplices were in jail. Newspaper headlines told the story.

'*The Best There Has Ever Been*'. That quote was from Kimi Hakkinen, the World Rally Champion. Below it was a picture of Robbie flying through the air at the bridge. But Robbie knew all that counted for nothing now. If he didn't win today then Keats would grab the headlines tomorrow.

Morning practice had gone well. The car was quick and handled perfectly. Now it was up to himself, Robbie knew. If he could take pole position, he felt confident he could win.

But his hopes were soon dashed. When he returned to the pits, he found his father in grim humour.

'What's wrong, Dad?' he asked.

'There's been an objection to you racing today,' Mr Scott said.

'What!' Robbie exclaimed. 'Why's there an objection?'

'Because you didn't inform the stewards yesterday that you weren't taking part in the race,' his father explained.

'But I couldn't inform them,' Robbie protested. 'Don't they know what happened yesterday? Don't they read the newspapers? It wasn't my fault.'

'I know,' his father said. 'But there are rules about not taking your place on the grid for a race. One of them states that you must inform the stewards if you're withdrawing. You didn't do so and now someone's lodged a protest against you taking part in today's race. They claim you should be disqualified.'

'It's Keats,' Robbie said bitterly. 'I'm going to sort him out.'

Robbie stormed off and found The Fox working on his car. He swung about when Robbie called his name.

'You can't win fairly, can you?' Robbie said. 'First you interfere with my car and now you lodge a protest against me with the stewards.'

The Fox stared at him as if he were crazy. 'I don't know what you mean,' he said. 'I've lodged no protest against you. And what's that about interfering with your car?'

'On Friday night someone swapped a faulty brake seal for a good one. It was why I crashed when qualifying.'

'And you're accusing me?' The Fox's face grew dark with rage. He rushed at Robbie and grappled with him. Mr Keats had to intervene. Then Mr Scott arrived.

Robbie had to repeat his accusations. Mr Keats became angry. 'None of us interfered with your car,' he said grimly. 'I would not tolerate such behaviour. But I saw one of Mr Marana's men coming from your garage Friday night. He must have swapped the seal.'

'But why would he do that?' Robbie said.

'At that time we were about to sign the sponsorship deal with him,' Mr Keats said. 'So Marana must have wanted to ensure that my son won the championship. If you were injured and couldn't take part in the races this weekend, then John would certainly win. As JFC Champion, he could travel freely all over the world. That way Marana could go on smuggling without any hindrance.'

'So who's made the protest, then?' Robbie asked.

'Timmy Morgan,' Mr Keats said.

Robbie grimaced. Morgan was the oldest driver of them all. He had always disliked being beaten by someone younger than him. This was his revenge for that.

'Look, I'm sorry for accusing you,' Robbie apologised. He held out his hand to The Fox. Keats hesitated, then shook Robbie's hand. Robbie also shook hands with Mr Keats.

'Good luck,' Mr Keats said. 'I hope you do race. I want my son to win fairly and beat the best there is. Then he can be a fitting champion.'

Robbie and his father returned to their garage. A steward was waiting for them.

'You must report to the Stewards' Office, Mr Scott,' he

said. 'A meeting to decide your son's fate is about to begin.'

Robbie couldn't bear to wait around so he went to see Sammy. She had been passed fit by the doctor and was going to race today. Even better news was that the owner of the stolen paintings had been so delighted to have them returned that he offered to be her sponsor.

Sammy, dressed in her overalls, was working on her kart. She smiled when she saw Robbie, but frowned when she saw his glum face.

'What's wrong?' she asked.

Quietly he told her. 'But that's so unfair,' she said.

'I know. And now Keats will win and be champion.'

'So what?' Sammy said. 'You're still the better driver. Would Keats have made that drive yesterday? Would he have got to me in time? You did Robbie. It was the greatest drive of your life.

'I know you want to be champion, Robbie. And one day you will be. One day you'll be a famous racing driver and the only foxes of note then will be those with long bushy tails.'

Robbie laughed and Sammy joined in. 'You mustn't blame yourself,' she said. 'It's all my fault really.'

'No!' Robbie exclaimed. 'You're not to blame. Now, let me help you and we'll say no more about it.'

Sammy and Robbie worked quietly, neither speaking. Time dragged slowly by. Each time Robbie looked at his watch, the hands had hardly moved. Finally he heard someone approach and he swung about. It was his father. He looked downcast.

Robbie's heart sank. He bit his lip and stared at the floor.

'I have good news and bad news,' Mr Scott said quietly. 'You can take part in the race, Robbie. But as a punishment for not reporting to the stewards yesterday, you must start from the back of the grid.'

Robbie and Sammy groaned. This decision, without doubt, would destroy Robbie's chance of winning. No one could start from the back of the grid and win. It had never been done. Now it was almost certain that The Fox would be crowned JFC Champion later today.

NINE

Despite starting from the rear of the field, the rules of the JFC stated that a driver had to qualify in order to take his place on the grid. This meant Robbie had to go through the qualifying session. In a way he was glad of that though. He would have hated to just sit around while the other drivers qualified.

Over the qualifying session, he and The Fox fought for the best time, lap by lap. This was one contest Robbie was determined to win. At least after the race, when The Fox was crowned champion, Robbie could be satisfied with the knowledge that he was the faster driver.

As Robbie began his final qualifying lap, The Fox led him by a tenth of a second. But Robbie drove what he considered his best lap ever. The car seemed to float above the track, drifting in and out of the corners, as if it were laser guided.

When he crossed the finishing line, Robbie knew he had smashed the lap record at Grange Park. He still had to start from the back of the grid, however. But he had beaten The Fox and now he began to believe he could even win the race.

His father was jubilant when Robbie returned to the pits.

'You've taken a whole second off the lap record,' he enthused. 'You're a far better driver than The Fox. You're more talented and quicker and much, much braver.' He put his arm about Robbie's shoulder. 'You'll be the World Champion one day, Robbie. Just you believe that.'

Robbie basked in his father's admiration. And then Sammy came to wish him luck.

'I know you can win this race, Robbie,' she said. 'You're a whole second per lap faster than The Fox. That's enough to catch him and beat him. Remember Robbie, you're the best driver in Ireland.'

Sammy's words of praise echoed in Robbie's head as he lined up at the back of the grid for the race. Today, he felt he could beat the whole world. His car was at its peak. He was driving better than he had ever driven before. He was ready.

The red lights went out. Eighteen racing engines screamed and tyres spun wildly, laying down burning rubber. Robbie made a brilliant start, streaking off the grid with a speed that defied the eye.

He split the two cars ahead of him and, leaving his braking to the last moment, passed a third car into Turn One. He could hear nothing above the roar of the engine and the whine of the wind. But he glimpsed the spectators from the corner of his eye and knew they were cheering wildly.

Robbie felt a surge of adrenaline. He really could catch The Fox and pass him. If he drove like he had yesterday, or this morning, it was certainly possible.

The laps reeled off one by one. Robbie gained four more places. He was now in among the faster cars. Overtaking became more difficult, but he gained time by slipstreaming the drivers. He cut The Fox's lead to ten seconds, then nine ... eight ...

At the halfway point he was in eighth place, seven seconds behind The Fox. And now that half his fuel was gone and the car was lighter, he was able to gain fractions of a second. As he passed the pits and saw his father hold up his timing board, he could hardly believe his eyes. He had just broken the lap record again.

On the next lap he gained a place and then, as two cars ahead vied with each other, Robbie slipped past them both on the straight. He was now in fifth position but what was better still, he was only six seconds behind The Fox.

The pressure was telling on the leading driver. He began to make small mistakes. At Turn One he ran wide and was almost taken by the second place car. He held on but lost valuable fractions of a second.

On the very next lap, Robbie broke the lap record again and grabbed fourth place. The car now seemed to have wings. A few laps later he took the third placed driver as if he were standing still. By the following lap he was in second place, flashing past his fellow competitor as they hurtled out of the final turn.

Robbie fairly flew down the straight. As he passed the pits his timing board told him there were five laps to go. The Fox's black car was just metres ahead of him now. The duel for first place was about to begin.

Robbie was an instinctive driver. But he had a brain too. He decided not to push The Fox at Turn One.

Instead he would push hard at the other turns and in the straight. This would lull his rival into a sense of false security. Then, when he wasn't expecting it, he'd take The Fox into Turn One on the second last lap.

The Fox swept into Turn One, taking a tight line. This left sufficient track for Robbie to overtake on the outside. It needed bravery and skill to do so, and Robbie lacked neither. But he stayed back, biding his time.

Approaching the first hairpin, Robbie jinxed right, then left and right again. It was impossible to overtake here, but he knew his manoeuvre would make The Fox think he was desperate to attack in such a place.

The Fox held the racing line, his speed on the short straight equal to Robbie's. The latter pressed again at the next hairpin; then at the series of turns which brought them back into the main straight.

Robbie was quicker out of the final turn. He got the nose of his car alongside his rival's rear wheels as they roared down the straight. But at Turn One he eased back into the leading car's wake.

The Fox's gloved fist gestured in triumph. Robbie smiled grimly. The Fox was overconfident, thinking Robbie would only attack him at the hairpins or the series of turns before the straight. When he realised what Robbie's intention was, it would be too late.

Robbie pressed again all through the next few laps. But his rival held the racing line and there was no opportunity to overtake. As they approached the final series of turns before the main straight, The Fox foolishly shook his fist again in triumph. It was sufficient to lose him fractions of a second.

As he swept out of the final turn Robbie was just inches from The Fox's exhaust. Then, slipstreaming him in the straight, Robbie suddenly swung out and drew alongside. They approached Turn One neck and neck at over 100 miles per hour.

The Fox's nerve broke first. He eased off the throttle. Robbie inched ahead. Then The Fox lost his nerve completely and braked. Robbie shot into the lead. But he had left his own braking very late. He was now turning into the bend. The car was travelling too fast. It was too close to the tyre barriers. Disaster was surely inevitable.

Robbie hit the brakes hard. The tyres locked, scorching the rubber so that smoke billowed out. The car began to slide sideways. Robbie's hands flicked the steering wheel to opposite lock, then back – left, then right and left again at a speed defying the human eye. Meanwhile, his foot beat a tattoo on the brake pedal as he tried to bring the car back under control.

As he fought the slewing car, he felt certain it was not even in contact with the track. Instead, it was floating an inch above the surface. In another moment it would smash sideways into the tyre barrier with a bone crunching impact.

In reality though, the tyres were up on the kerb and the car mere inches from the barrier when Robbie managed to regain control. Then, flooring the throttle, he roared out of the turn. He was through. He was leading. Even above the engine noise and the wind, he thought he heard the cheers of the crowd.

But he couldn't afford to lose concentration – not now. The Fox was on his tail. Even the tiniest mistake could cost him the race and the championship. Totally focused, Robbie held the racing line for the remainder of the lap and then for the final one.

Sweeping out of the last turn and into the straight, he saw the chequered flag ahead. Clenched fist raised, he crossed the finishing line. Robbie had achieved the impossible. He had come from the back of the field to beat his greatest rival. Now he knew for certain he could be a great racing champion one day.

He glimpsed his father on the pit wall along with Sammy. Both were waving madly. Further on, Mr Pearce sat in his wheelchair, fists clenched in triumph. Robbie saluted them, waving his clenched fist.

He completed his victory lap, revelling in his success. At the end of the lap, Robbie returned to the pits to be hugged by his father.

'You're going to be the greatest champion of them all,' Bob Scott said. 'I'm so proud of you today, Robbie. You've driven the race of a lifetime.'

Sammy shook Robbie's hand, her face beaming. Her father grabbed Robbie's hand in both of his. 'You're a fitting champion, Robbie,' he said. 'No one else could have achieved what you have today.'

Suddenly Robbie was surrounded by the other competitors. The Fox was among them. They all shook Robbie's hand and congratulated him. Then, before Robbie realised what was happening, they hoisted him shoulder high and carried him to the top step of the podium.

'Ladies and gentlemen,' the JFC President said, 'we have seen here today a truly great racing champion.

Against all the odds, Robbie Scott has come from the back of the grid to win. That takes guts, courage and immense skill. But it takes a belief in yourself too.'

'Today, Robbie has shown he has that belief. Without it, he would not have won. It has been an honour for all of us gathered here to witness a true champion and a magnificent win. Now it gives me great pleasure to congratulate him and present him with his trophy. It is not his first, and it will not be his last. Ladies and gentlemen, I give you the Irish JFC Champion and a future Formula One World Champion ... Of that I have no doubt.'

The President shook Robbie's hand and presented him with the large silver cup. As Robbie took it and raised it aloft, he sought his father among the cheering crowd below the podium. When he picked him out, he stooped down.

Bob Scott wiped his eyes. Then he caught Robbie in an embrace. His father was shaking with emotion but Robbie didn't care. This was their day and he had never before known such happiness.